Fancy NANCY
and the Posh Puppy

Written by
Jane O'Connor

Illustrated by
Robin Preiss Glasser

HarperCollins *Children's Books*

First published in hardback in the U.S.A by HarperCollins Publishers Inc in 2007
First published in paperback in Great Britain by HarperCollins Children's Books in 2008

3 5 7 9 10 8 6 4

ISBN- 13 978-0-00-725483-5

HarperCollins Children's Books is a division of HarperCollins Publishers Ltd.

Text copyright © Jane O'Connor 2007
Illustrations copyright © Robin Preiss Glasser 2007

Typography by Jeanne L. Hogle

Visit our website: www.harpercollins.co.uk

Printed in China

For Margaret Anastas, an absolute firecracker of an editor, all my thanks
for ushering Nancy into the world and making the whole experience so much fun
—J.O'C.

For my agent and friend, Faith Hamlin, who has doggedly helped me
through thick and thin
—R.P.G.

I am ecstatic. (That's a fancy word for happy.)
We're going to get a puppy – a real one.

I hope we get a papillon, like our neighbour's dog. You say it like this: *pappy-yon.* In French it means butterfly.

I help Mrs DeVine take care of Jewel.

We take her to the beauty salon.

We buy her new ensembles.
(That's a fancy word for clothes.)

Papillons are so posh.
(That's a fancy word for fancy.)

There is only one problem . . . my parents.
"Papillons like to stay indoors," my dad says.
"They're too little."

"And delicate," my mum says.
"What about one of these dogs?"

I shake my head. Too big. Too brown. Too plain.
Sometimes it's hard being the only fancy person in a family.

Then I get an idea that is spectacular.
(That's a fancy word for great.)
We can puppy-sit for Jewel!

My parents say OK.
So does Mrs DeVine.
My family will see how happy we'll
be with a papillon puppy.

I introduce Jewel to my doll, Marabelle.

I show my sister how
to groom Jewel . . .

. . . and how to scoop
her poop.

My sister wants to hold and kiss Jewel.

I tell her, "You must be gentle."

"What a responsible girl you are," my mum says.
"Some dog is going to be very lucky."

"Merci," I say. (That's French for "thank you.")

Two of my friends are walking their dogs.
"Come over to my house," I say. "I'm puppy-sitting.
All the dogs can play together."

Rusty splashes in the paddling pool.
Jewel hides behind my legs.

Scamp plays fetch.

"Go, Jewel. Go get the ball!" I yell.
Jewel just looks at me.

"She gets exhausted pretty quickly,"
I tell my friends. (That's a fancy word
for tired.)

While Jewel gets her beauty
rest, we have refreshments.

Oh, no! Look what my sister is doing.
Poor Jewel is terrified!

"Mum! Come quick. Jewel is going to be sick!"

"When we get our papillon,
I'm not letting her near it," I say.

My mum whispers, "She doesn't know better.
She was trying to be nice."
I know that.

We take Jewel back to her house.
She is a perfect dog for Mrs DeVine.
But maybe she isn't the perfect dog for us.

I'm so sad I hardly get fancy when we go to the King's Crown for dinner.

La Salle Street Animal Shelter

On the way home, we drive by the animal shelter.
"Let's take a look," my mum says. "All those dogs need
a family to love them."

I ask the lady, "Are there any fancy dogs here?"
And she says, "I think I have just the dog for you. She's funny
and playful and smart and cuddly. Her name is Frenchy."

Hmmmm . . . Frenchy? I like the sound of that.

Frenchy runs right to me and jumps in my lap.
She likes it when my sister hugs her.

Frenchy is the perfect dog for us.

My dad says Frenchy is a La Salle spaniel. That is a very unique breed. (Unique is fancy for one of a kind.)

You know what?
Maybe that's even better than fancy.